**9** LITTLE BASH STREET KIDS SWINGING ON A GATE —

SIDNEY GOT HIS HEAD STUCK FAST, THEN THERE WERE..... **8**

ATTY SWALLOWED FAR TOO MUCH, THEN THERE WERE..... **7**

LITTLE BASH STREET KIDS GOING FOR A DRIVE —

SPOTTY'S TIE CAUGHT ON A THORN, THEN THERE WERE..... **5**

. C. Thomson & Co., Ltd., 1987.
ISBN 0-85116-386-6.

**TURN TO INSIDE BACK COVER**

**£2.85**

# DENNIS the MENACE and GNASHER in–
## "THE GREAT SLEDGE RACE" PART 1

EITHER GNASHER'S AGED SUDDENLY, OR IT'S SNOWING!

HAW-HAW!

YAHOO! SNOW AT LAST! MUST GET MY SLEDGE OUT!

TUG

TOY CUPBOARD

TOPPLE

FLOP!

THE SNOW WILL BE FOLLOWED BY A SUDDEN THAW

ZOOM!

I WARNED YOU!

SUDDEN THAW

SUDDEN THAW

CLUNK!

ERK!

BOUNCE

BOUNCE

FLOP!

KEEN TO SEE THE FOOTBALL RESULTS, ARE YOU, DENNIS?

I HOPE THIS IS OUR PAPER!

DAZED

COO! I'D BE ABLE TO USE MY SLEDGE THERE!

DAILY BLAH

BRITAIN SEEKS ENTRANT FOR ARCTIC SLEDGE RACE

YOU'LL DO GNASHER, BUT IT'LL TAKE MORE THAN YOU TO MAKE A SLEDGE DOG TEAM!

ZOOM!

ZOOOM!

So——

SLEDGE DOGS WANTED

MUST BE BRAVE, INTELLIGENT AND ABLE TO WITHSTAND THE COLD.

STOP HERE, PALS!

ARE YOU ABLE TO STAND THE COLD?

EH?

STOP ME and BUY ONE

WAH! MY ICE CREAM! RUINED!

YES — YOU DO LIKE COLD THINGS!

Next —

NOW TO GET THE SUPPLIES ABOARD, AND THEN . . .

BEANO

CRISPS

AHA! I COULD USE SOME EXTRA MONEY— I'M BROKE!

HOTEL

ODD JOB BOY WANTED

WAH! THE DOOR WON'T STOP GOING ROUND!

HOTEL

ODD JOB BOY WANTED

ZOOM!

W-WOW! I'M A MINI-WHIZZ WHIRLWIND!

WHOOSH!

Then—

I HOPE THEIR PERMS AREN'T TOO EXPENSIVE!

SPIN-N

OPEN

HAIR STYLIST

YEEK!

GOSH! MY HAIR'S PERFECTLY PERMED!

HAIR STYLIST

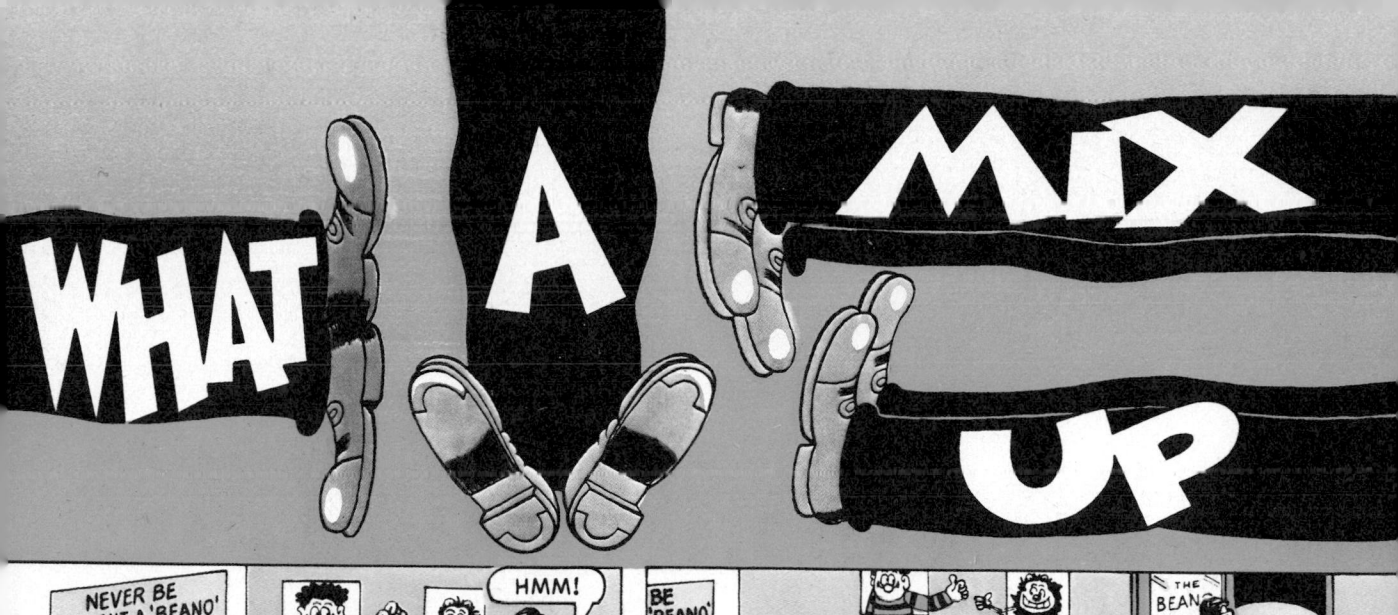

LOOKS BORING TO ME! BETTER LIVEN THIS UP!

BIT CHOPPY TODAY, EH, SKIPPER?

OOPS! MAN OVERBOARD!

GLURG!

KRUMP!

HAVE A LIFEBELT!

PLOP!

LEAVE ME ALONE!

BUT WHAT YOU'RE DOING IS BORING!

This is a full-page comic strip.

**Panel 1:** GLUB! · SPLOOSH!

**Panel 2:** WAVES GETTING HIGH, ARE THEY? · I BET YOU'RE TO BLAME! COUGH!

**Panel 3:** LOOK OUT — IT'S THE Q.E.2! · YEEK! · PARP! PARP!

**Panel 4:** I'M SWITCHING TO THE EXERCISE BIKE AND I WANT NO PRANKS! · ME?

**Panel 5:** I THINK I'LL MAKE IT MORE REALISTIC!

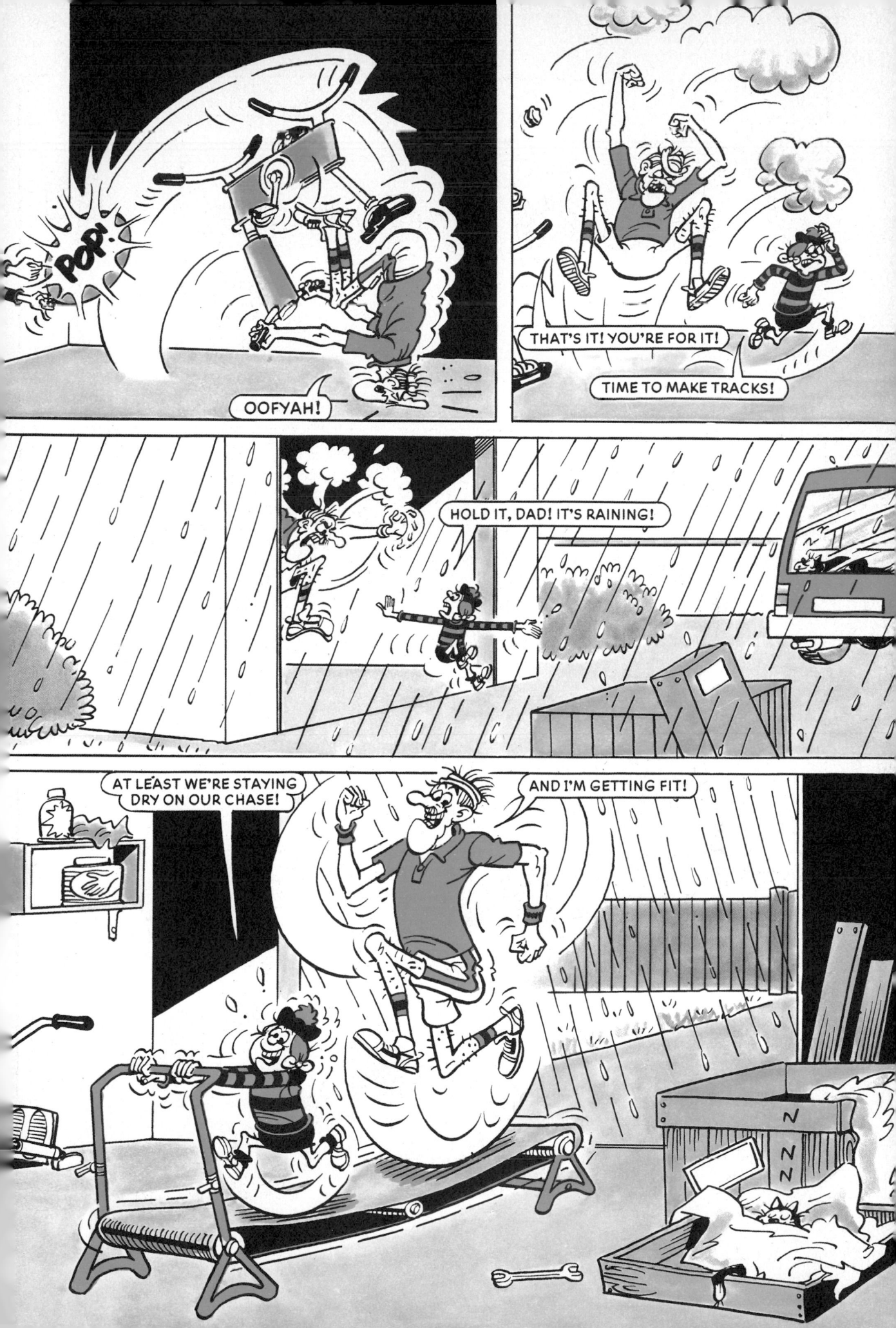

# THE BASH STREET KIDS

BEHAVE, OR . . .

OR WHAT, TEACHER?

SPLAT

PUSH

PLOP!

YOU'LL GET LINES!

I MUST BEHAVE IN CLASS

YAWN!

YAWN, BORING! WE ALWAYS GET LINES!

**Panel 1:**

WAIT FOR IT! CHUCKLE!

GRAB

**Panel 2:**

HEH! HEH!

**Panel 3:**

SPLAT

URK!

GASP! I DIDN'T EXPECT THAT!

**Panel 4:**

GO TO THE CANTEEN AND MARRY A POTATO!

GLOOP!

GASP! I DIDN'T EXPECT _THAT_!

**Panel 5:**

I TAKE THIS POTATO TO BE MY LAWFUL WEDDED SPUD!

POTATO WITH WEDDING VEIL ON

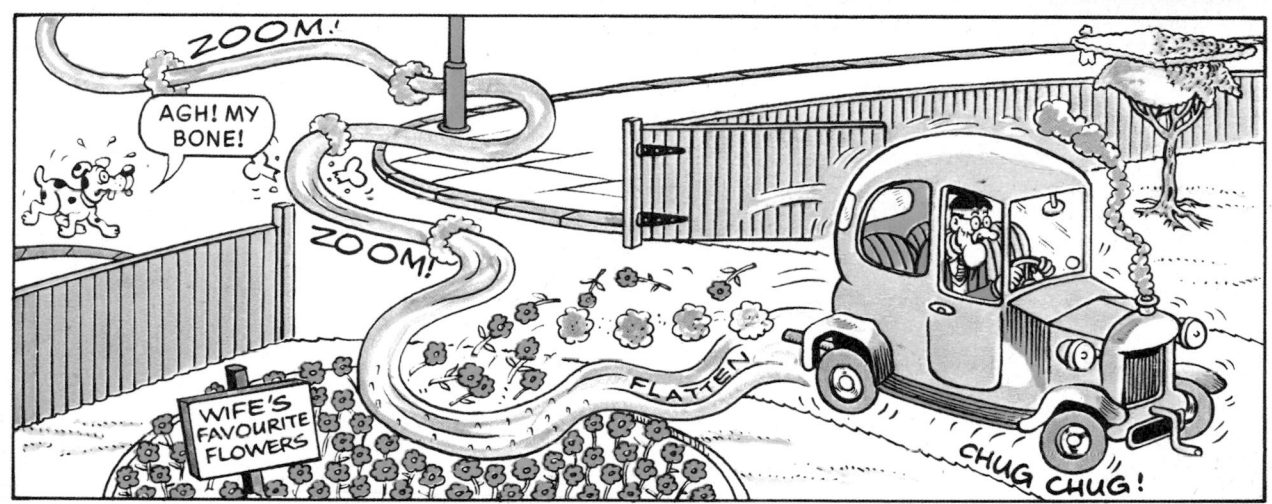

# BIFFO the BEAR

# TOM, DICK and SALLY

OO! YOUR UNCLES ARE HERE FROM AUSTRALIA — HAVEN'T SEEN THEM IN YEARS!

NOD! NOD!

BNO 1

HI, SIS — WE'VE BROUGHT YOU A PRESENT.

GROAN! THEY HAVEN'T CHANGED.

SPRING!

AREN'T THEY GREAT?

LET'S HAVE AFTERNOON TEA.

JAM

WHAP!

"LAND YOUR FIST ON WALTER'S NOSE", IT'S CALLED!

COME WITH ME, WORM!

THIS IS CALLED "DROP THE WORM IN DAD'S MOUTH"!

SNORE!

ZZZZ!

GASP! JUST IN TIME!

I MUST PUT A STOP TO ALL THIS NONSENSE!

SCREAM! Y-ELL!

THIS IS CALLED "PUT THE TAIL ON THE IVY"! PONY TAIL, THAT IS!

LET ME GO!

PUP PARADE
with the
BASH STREET PUPS
TAIL SALE
Wah! I've lost mine!
You're sitting on it, idiot!
We need new tails- ours are pretty puny!
Would sir care to try this magician's dog's tail?
How does it work?
WAG
Wow! Now I see!
POP!

Cowboys' dogs use this one!

I like it! I like it!

GLURK!

It's a bit droopy! What kind is it?

I'll show you!

A snake-charmer's dog's tail! Super!

Arf-arf!

COFFEE

What kind should I get, mister?

The bird-watcher's dog's variety!

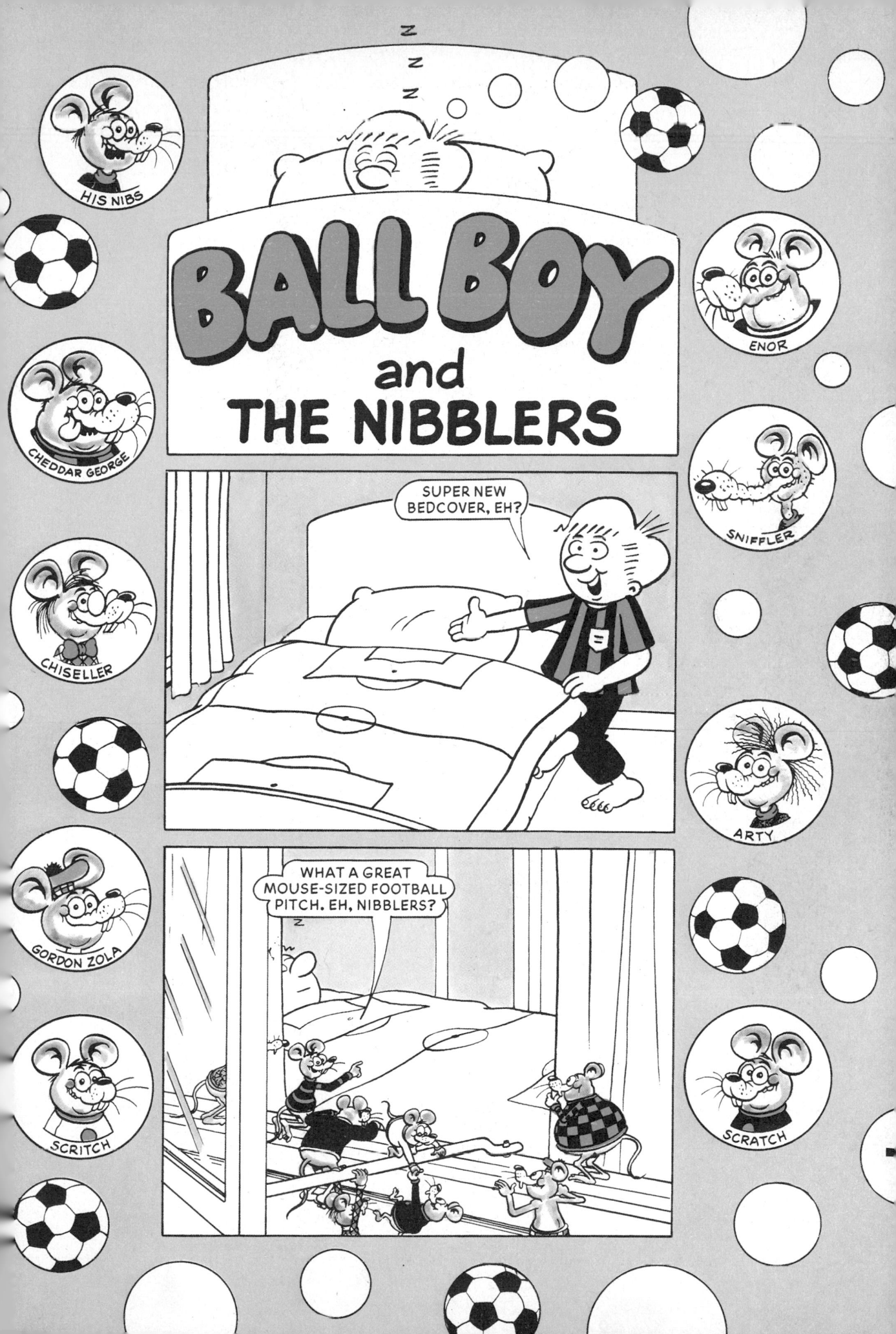

HMM . . . WE DON'T HAVE A BALL.

LOOK WHAT I FOUND.

PERFECT!

ALL WE NEED NOW ARE GOALPOSTS.

HERE'S ONE SET.

EH? WH-WHAT'S HAPPENING?

I THOUGHT I SAW MICE ALL OVER MY BED.

IT MUST HAVE BEEN A DREAM — I'LL HAVE TO STOP EATING CHEESE BEFORE BEDTIME!

THAT'S ODD — I DIDN'T HAVE CHEESE FOR SUPPER.

**GNASHER'S TALE**

I WAS ONCE BEHIND BARS...

I'M IN PRISON!

GNMM...ICICLES!

ROAR!

THESE COULD BE USEFUL...

# GNASHER'S Holiday SNAPS

# LORD SNOOTY

WHAT'S HE UP TO NOW?

I'M TRYING TO CATCH THIS PINCUSHION.

I THINK I'LL CATCH SOMETHING ELSE NOW.

WHAT BAIT WILL YOU USE?

BREAD AND JAM.

JAM

I'M FLY FISHING — AND LOOK AT THE SUPER FLIES I'VE CAUGHT!

BUZZ

BUZZ

# FORBIDDEN DODGES

THESE BOOKS ARE GREAT FOR DAY-TO-DAY DODGES!

BUT FOR REALLY DESPERATE SITUATIONS . . .

. . . I'VE GOT THIS "FORBIDDEN DODGES" DODGE BOOK!

I ONLY OPEN THIS BOOK IN EMERGENCIES. THE DODGES IN HERE ARE TOO DANGEROUS TO USE OFTEN!

GASP! DIDN'T KNOW YOU HAD A BOOK LIKE THAT!

READER

I'VE BEEN MAKING MYSELF A DRESS! YOU CAN MODEL IT WHILE I MAKE ALTERATIONS!

HORROR OF HORRORS!

D-DON'T OPEN THAT BOOK, ROGER! USE A NORMAL DODGE!

SO...

I'VE HAD A BAG OF APPLES, MUM. I'M TOO FAT TO BE A MODEL!

THAT'S OK, THEN! PHEW!

HEH! HEH! I DIDN'T SAY I'D EATEN THEM!

LET US SEE WHAT'S IN THIS GREAT "FORBIDDEN DODGES" BOOK, ROGER!

IT'S VERY RISKY, PALS . . .

TREMBLE!

BOOM!

H-HERE GOES!

SEE WHAT'S HAPPENED WHEN HE OPENED THE BOOK.

BOOM!

DANGER QUARRY

DODGED THEM! THE BOOM CAME FROM THERE, AND THIS BOOK STAYS SHUT!

ROGER'S DODGE-CLINIC

SPECIAL OFFER FOR "BEANO" CHARACTERS ONLY

AH! HERE'S IVY. ISN'T SHE CUTE?

WHAT CAN I DO FOR YOU, DEAR?

I WANT A DODGE TO MAKE ME TOUGHER!

I DON'T HAVE ONE — SHE'S TOUGH ENOUGH AS IT IS!

OINK! SNURFLE! SNORK! GRUNTLE!

AH! YOU WANT A DODGE TO GET MORE SWILL, RASHER!

PIG DODGES

ROGER! HERE'S YOUR...

TRIP!

...LUNCH! OOPS!

SPLAT!

HMPH! MY LUNCH IS RASHER'S SWILL, NOW!

GUZZLE! SLURP! CHOMP

HOW CAN I DODGE BEING SO UNLUCKY?

SLAM!

CRASH!

SWING!

WATCH THE DOOR, JAMES — TOO LATE!

CRASH!

GROAN! IT'S FAR TOO DANGEROUS HAVING A CLINIC FOR "BEANO" CHARACTERS!

JUST MY LUCK! HIT BY THE BIGGEST BOOK ON THE SHELF!

ARGH! LOOK AT ALL THESE TERRORS STILL TO COME!

NEXT TWO PLEASE!

CRASH!

JAM!

THAT'S US!

WEDGE!

LUCKILY I SAVED A DODGE FOR THE MOST IMPORTANT BEANO CHARACTER OF ALL — ME! I'M OFF!

STUCK!

# WHO'S WON THE CUP?

HERE GOES . . .

DIS IS ROGER. I CAN'T CUB TO SCHOOL. GOT A BAD COLD ID BY DOSE!

NOT BAD, BUT IT DOESN'T WIN!

NEED A BETTER DODGE TO WIN THAT TROPHY . . .

HERE'S A GREAT DODGE TO HIDE YOUR "BEANO" FROM YOUR DAD IF YOU DON'T WANT HIM TO READ IT!

BUT I DON'T SEE ANY "BEANO"!

SHOWS YOU WHAT A GOOD HIDING PLACE THIS IS!

YES — BUT IT'S NOT DODGE OF THE YEAR!

AW! HE'S TAKING IT BADLY!

SOB!

AHA! JUST THE WATER PISTOL DODGE!

DO I GET THE PRIZE?

YES — A SURPRIZE!

DAD

DAD'S TRICKED ME INTO GIVING AWAY SOME TOP DODGES!

NEVER MIND, YOU DO WIN A TROPHY . . .

BAH! I'VE WON THE DAFT DODGER OF THE YEAR AWARD!

DAFT DODGER

# BRINGING UP GNIPPER

TODAY I'M GOING TO TEACH YOU THE TRICKS OF THE DOGGIE TRADE!

RIGHT, DAD!

FIRST, BONE BURYING. READY, GNIPPER?

WAIT TILL DAD'S PLANTING ROSES TO SAVE HAVING TO DIG A HOLE YOURSELF!

SWEAT

PUFF! PANT!

CEMENT →

ER — BUT MAKE SURE DAD'S NOT CEMENTING IN FENCE POSTS INSTEAD!

SCRAPE!

SCRAPE AT THE DOOR TO GET INTO THE HOUSE!

HIDE WHEN DAD COMES TO THE DOOR!

THEN SNEAK IN WHEN HE'S NOT LOOKING...

...SO YOU CAN GET THE BEST CHAIR IN THE HOUSE!

YIP! YIP!

BUT BE SURE DAD SEES YOU WHEN HE GETS BACK!

SQUASH!

YEEK!

NO, GNIPPER. YOU'LL GET FAT!

WIDE EYED LOOK

IF YOU WANT SCRAPS FROM THE TABLE, FIRST TRY THE APPEALING LOOK!

IF THAT FAILS TO WORK...

... PULL THE TABLE CLOTH OFF THE TABLE...

TUG

ZOOM!

... MAKING SURE TO AVOID A BOWL OF MUM'S CUSTARD!

PLOP!

HERE'S HOW TO GET A WALK!

OO! DALLASTY! MY FAVOURITE!

CLICK!

OH, NO!

I'M NOT WATCHING THAT. I'M GOING OUT FOR A WALK!

YOU CAN KEEP MUM COMPANY WHILE I'M OUT!

YEEK!

HERE'S ANOTHER TIP...

GNUP! GNUP!

...KEEP CLEAR OF ANGRY PUPS WHO DON'T LIKE YOUR ADVICE!

# MONSTER MIRTH

**PUNYCORN**

CANDY FLOSS

EVERYTHING'S BIGGER OVER HERE — MUST HAVE A WATER MELON.

PUT THAT GRAPE DOWN!

GRAB

ER . . . SEE WHAT I MEAN?

SINCE I'M IN FLORIDA, I MUST VISIT THE ALLIGATOR WRESTLING.

BABY WORLD ALLIGATOR WRESTLING 3·00 p.m DAILY

HMPH! NOT MUCH FUN WHEN IT'S A BABY ALLIGATOR!

ALLIGATOR EGG

GHOST TRAIN

THE TRAIN'S GOING TO START NOW!

THIS GHOST TRAIN LOOKS INTERESTING.

TOTTER!

WHEEZE!

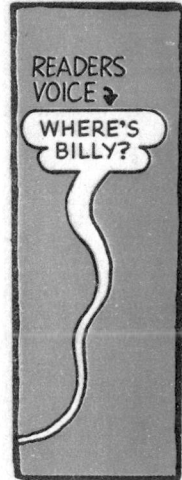

READERS VOICE →

WHERE'S BILLY?

ER — HERE I AM! I THINK ALL THAT WHIZZING ABOUT HAS AGED ME!

GASP! ERM — WANT A GAME OF FOOTBALL, BILLY?

OH, DEAR! HE MIGHT FALL AND HURT HIS OLD BONES!

WHEEZE! PUFF!

TOTTER!

THIS IS MORE YOUR SPEED, I THINK!

WHEEZE!

RASP!

SOB! WHAT'S HAPPENED TO YOU, BILLY? YOU USED TO BURN UP THE PAGES!

A BILLY WHIZZ FAN

# PUP PARADE

Ah, almost bone time! Sigh!

And here they are! Slurp!

You get your bones too easily – you could do with working off some flab!

Earn your bones with the puzzles I've set you over the page.

ANSWER
THIRTEEN BONES

Did you count them all readers? Check your answer up above! Phew!

# TRIVIAL BONES

**FOOD** ARE THERE ANY BONES IN CARROT SOUP?

**HISTORY** IS THERE A PLACE CALLED BONEHENGE?

**ART** DID FRED BLOGGS PAINT THE BONA LISA?

**SPORT** DO OXFORD AND CAMBRIDGE COMPETE IN THE BONE RACE?

Groan! I hope you answered "NO" to all the questions, readers.

THE PUPS HAVE TO FIND A SAFE ROUTE TO THE OTHER SIDE OF THE POND. HELP THEM, READERS —

OTHER SIDE

MONSTER MIRTH

PIGASUS

ENTRY FORM ................

CONTEST ................

CONTESTANT ................

# MINNIE THE MINX

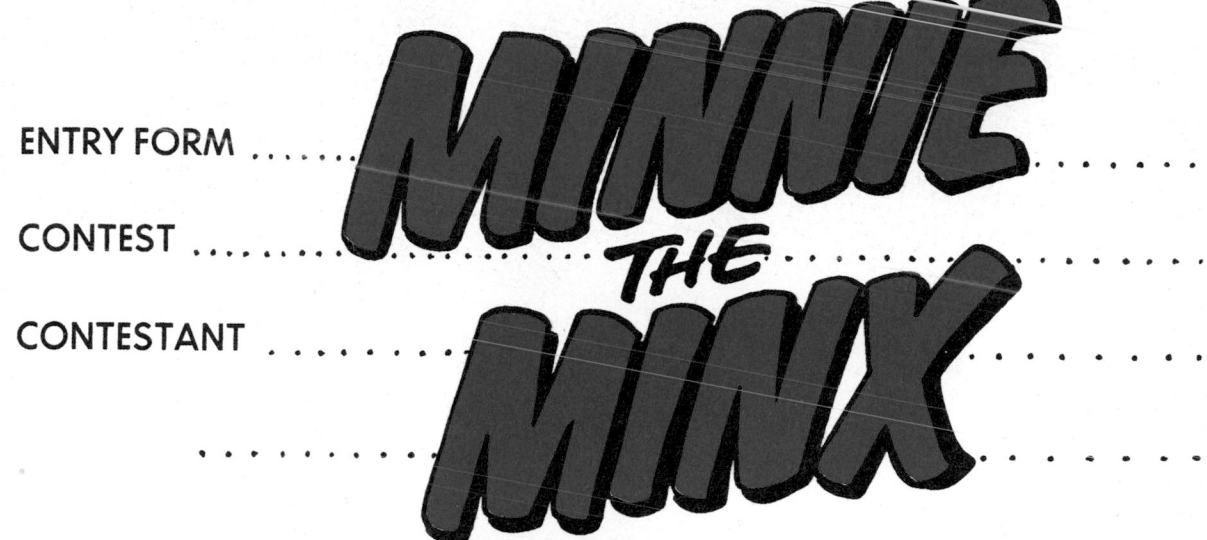

FIRST — THE "EATING A PACKET OF DRY CRACKERS IN ONE MINUTE" CONTEST!

CRACKERS

CRACKERS

CRACKERS

VERY DRY CHEWS

IT'S IMPOSSIBLE, READERS! TRY IT! HEE-HEE!

OSTRICH CONTEST! GO!

YOU'VE WON, P.C. TYME! CHUCKLE! HE CAN'T HEAR ME!

MIN'S SAND PIT.

SHATTER!

WE'RE IN THE TAP-DANCING CONTEST!

SHATTER!

THUMP!

CLUMP!

I'M WINNING THE BEAVER CONTEST!

CHOMP!

INDIAN ELEPHANTS MUST EAT CURRY.

EXTRA STRONG CURRY

STEAMING CURRY SMELL

SUCK! SUCK! SUCK!

GROO!

YEEOW!

ARGH!

MUST HAVE WATER! GASP!

ERK!

# DON'T SAY THAT!

## Things not to mention

ANYONE SEEN MY PET TARANTULA?

... IN THE STREET—

CALL ME A TAXI!

OK — YOU'RE A TAXI!

... WHEN SOMEONE'S EATING SPAGHETTI—

LIKE TO SEE MY WORM COLLECTION?

HERE ARE YOUR TICKETS FOR THE CLASS DANCE, IN THE SCHOOL HALL, AT SEVEN O'CLOCK TONIGHT!

CLASS IIB

FLIP

GRAB DANCE

So—

YEH, LET'S DANCE!

SNAP SNAP

SCHOOL DANCE Tonight

BASH ST. SCHOOL

WHERE DO YOU UNRULY MOB THINK YOU'RE GOING?

SHOW TICKETS AT DOOR

SCHOOL HALL

IT'S ME, TEACHER!

AARGH! SO IT IS! KEEP THOSE DARK GLASSES ON!

PUSH

I THOUGHT THIS MIGHT HAPPEN! CHANGE INTO THESE EXTRA SCHOOL UNIFORMS!

KIDS' SCHOOL UNIFORMS

HUH! SOME DANCE THIS IS GOING TO BE.

VERY LOUD POP MUSIC

EEAGH!

YOU CAN'T DANCE TO THAT MUSIC . . .

TWOINNG!

SNIP

TWOING

SNIP

YE GRAMOPHONE

WIND

PATHETIC

TERRY BULL

AWFUL

−O +O

TIME FOR A GAME!

HMMM . . .

CLICK!

WE'LL PLAY AT THE GHOSTS OF BASH STREET . . .

THAT'S NOT A PARTY GAME . . .

CLICK!

AW, NO!

WHIRL!

RING-A-RING
A ROSES...

SPIN

TEACHER, TEACHER! THIS
ISN'T THE KIND OF
DANCE ANYBODY LIKES
NOWADAYS!

OH, ISN'T IT,
HEAD?

CLASS
II B

KISS ME

BLAST
OF POP
MUSIC

DONK

SPIN

HOOCH
KOOCH

DOO-A-DEE DEE!

THROW

GOOD RHYTHM,
SMIFFY!

WELL, IF YOU CAN'T
BEAT THEM!

THIS IS OUR NEW SIGNING. CHICO, FROM BRAZIL.

GOOD PLAYER, EH?

GREAT CONTROL

SWERVE!

BEND!

SWERVE!

BOOT!

AND HE CAN BEND THE BALL.

DIZZY SWOON!

GOAL!

# IVY the TERRIBLE

TOLD YOU, IVY!

URK! I'M DOWN INSTEAD!

RIGHT, YOU!

YOU'LL STAY DOWN THIS TIME!

AARGH!

BIFF!

...oon—
I'M SURE HE WILL!
HE DEFINITELY WON'T GET UP THIS TIME!
BASH!
THUMP!
AMAZING! I THOUGHT THOSE THINGS ALWAYS ROCKED BACK UP AGAIN!
TOLD YOU, MUM!
MUST ADMIT MY CHEWING GUM WAS A BIG HELP, THOUGH!
SHLUCK!

HERE I GO!

HI, READERS!

Suddenly —

CLICK!

BIFFO

AHEM! I HAD THE FILM IN BACKWARDS!

HAR-HAR-HAR!

COULD YOU ... WHISPER, WHISPER ...

TURN

PHEEP!

LITTLE RED RIDING HOOD. WE WOLVES HAVE GOT A BONE TO PICK WITH HER!

STOP! STOP!

THUNDER OF PAWS

VLADIVOSTOCK! IT'S GNASHER!

THAT'S THEM OUT OF THE WAY!

OOYAH!

JAM

I'LL PUT DENNIS OUT OF THE RACE!

SAW!

ICE BOOMERANG

THROW

YAH! MISSED!

DUCK

SPLAT!

PTCHEEE!

YOU MISSED ME, ANYWAY!

YOU'VE UPSET OUR CHINESE PAL, THOUGH!

CHOP!

CHOP!

YOU COULD WIN A T-SHIRT LIKE THIS BY WRITING TO DENNIS'S CLUB PAGE! SEE WEEKLY 'BEANO' FOR DETAILS!

 LITTLE BASH STREET KIDS WALKING BY THE SHORE –

CUTHBERT 'FELL' INTO A POOL, THEN THERE WERE.....

 LITTLE BASH STREET KIDS ARE OFFERED OLIVE'S STEW –

STUPID SMIFFY ATE THE LOT, THEN THERE WERE.....

 LITTLE BASH STREET KID BUYS FISH AND CHIPS AND THEN,